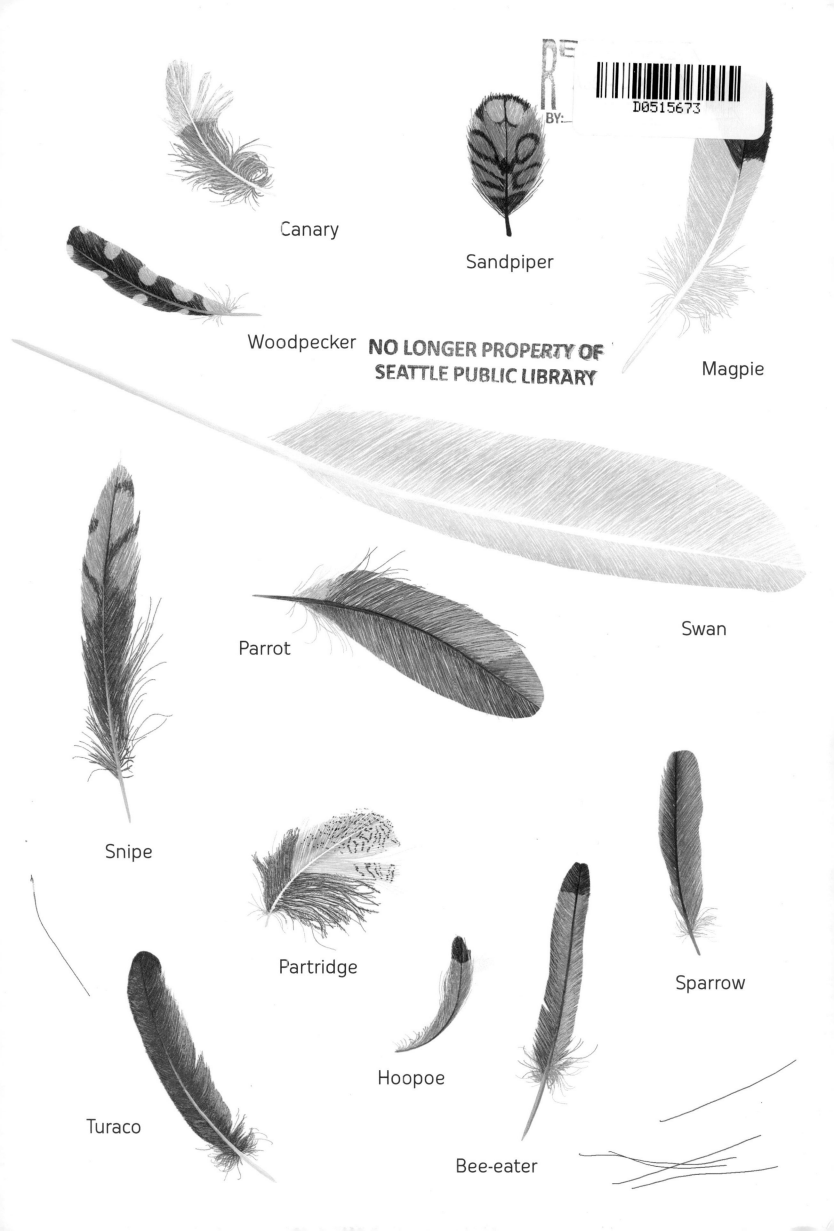

Canary

Sandpiper

Woodpecker

Magpie

Swan

Parrot

Snipe

Partridge

Sparrow

Hoopoe

Turaco

Bee-eater

for Robinson

First published in the United States in 2017
by Eerdmans Books for Young Readers,
an imprint of Wm. B. Eerdmans Publishing Co.
2140 Oak Industrial Dr. NE
Grand Rapids, Michigan 49505
www.eerdmans.com/youngreaders

Originally published in France in 2012 under the title *Plume*
by Éditions courtes et longues, Paris
Text and illustrations by Isabelle Simler

© Éditions courtes et longues, 2012

English language translation © 2017 Eerdmans Books for Young Readers

Manufactured at Tien Wah Press in Malaysia.

23 22 21 20 19 18 17   9 8 7 6 5 4 3 2 1

ISBN 978-0-8028-5492-6

A catalog listing is available from the Library of Congress.

The illustrations were created digitally.
The type was set in Oceania.

MIX
Paper from
responsible sources
FSC® C012700
FSC
www.fsc.org

Plume

Isabelle Simler

Eerdmans Books for Young Readers

Grand Rapids, Michigan

Goose

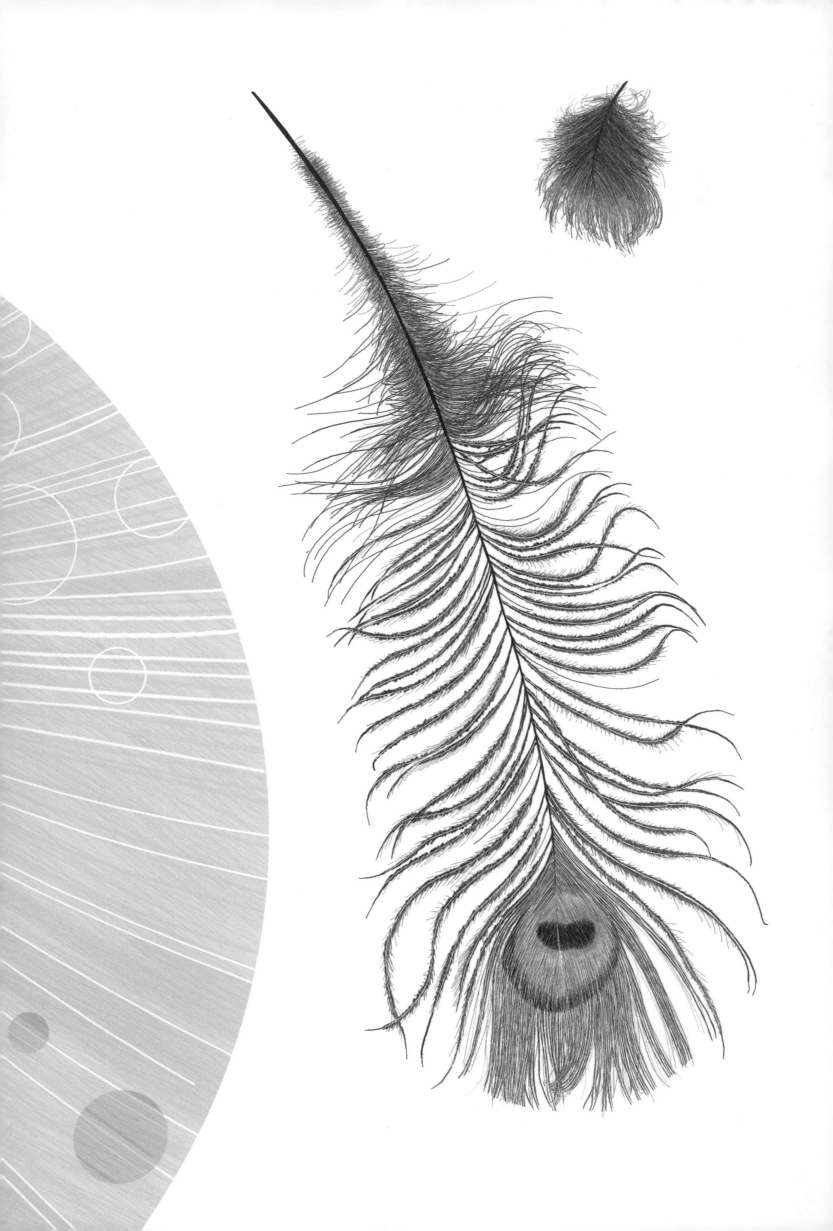

Peacock

Seagull

Ibis

Nuthatch

Guinea fowl

Owl

Stork

Eagle

Blackbird

Kingfisher

Jay

Parrotfinch

Pigeon

Turkey

Swallow

Chicken

Duck

oh . . . me? . . .
I collect feathers . . .

Cat

. . . because I love overstuffed pillows.

I am a dreamer cat.

They call me Plume.

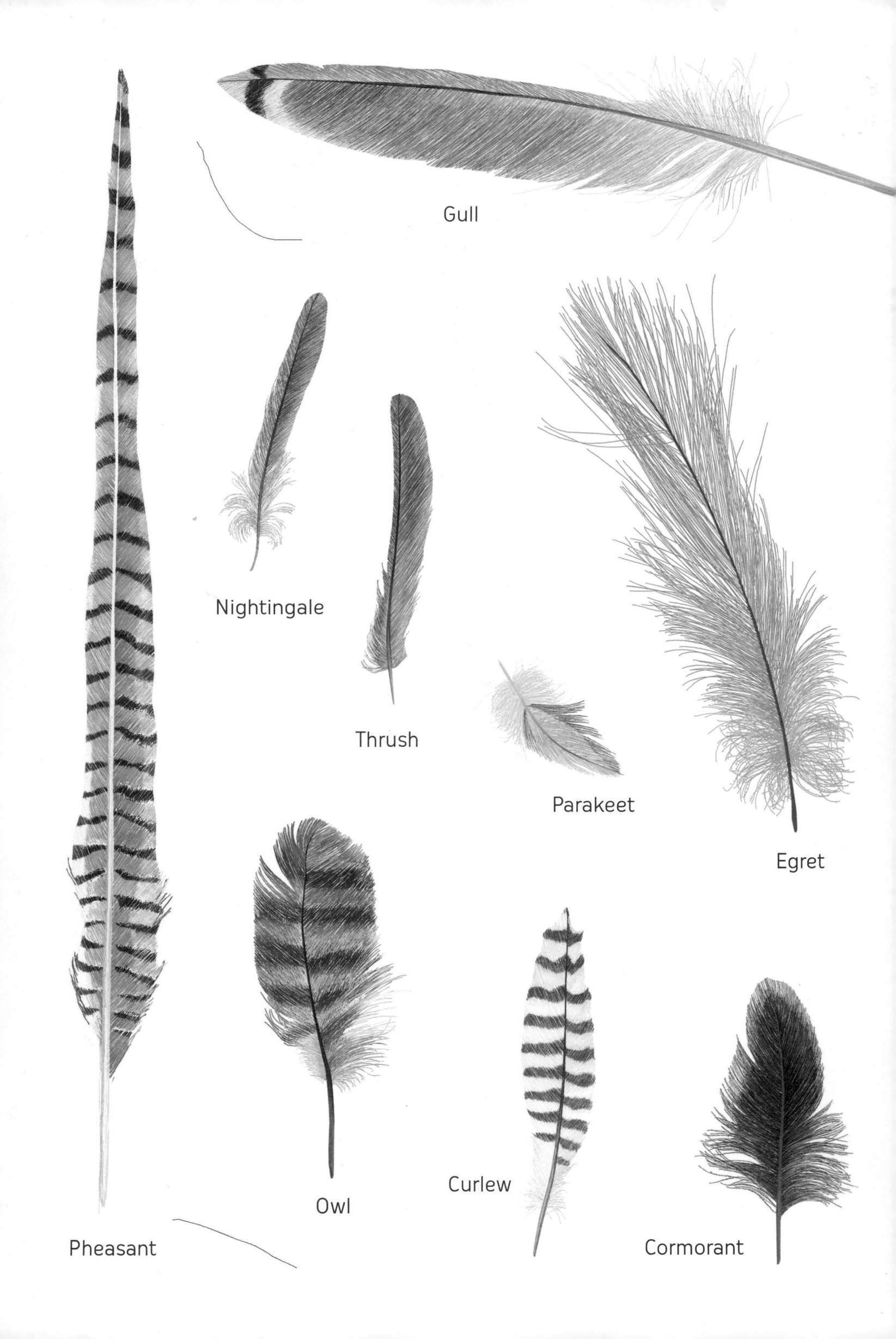

Gull

Nightingale

Thrush

Parakeet

Egret

Pheasant

Owl

Curlew

Cormorant